DISNEY PRINCESS

Cinderella

THE LITTLE MERMAID

Movie Theater Storybook & Movie Projector®

Adapted by Judy Katschke

Illustrated by Disney Storybook Artists

CONTENTS

Reader's Digest Children's Books®

Pleasantville, New York • Montréal, Québec • Bath, United Kingdom

Cinderella

DISK 1
I

Once upon a time, there was a lovely young girl who lived with her widowed father.

She was happy and kind to all. However, her father felt that she needed a mother, and in time he married a woman with two young daughters of her own.

When her dear father died, the young girl soon learned the true natures of her cruel stepmother and stepsisters. They called her Cinderella and forced her to do all the work of the household. She sang as she cooked and cleaned and never complained

about her hard life. Cinderella dreamed
that someday the wishes dear to her heart
would come true, and she would find true
love and happiness. The barnyard animals

became her
companions,
and she was so
gentle that even
the birds and
mice did not
fear her.

Gus and Jaq were two mice that Cinderella fed and dressed. They loved her dearly and wished they could do something to help her.

One day, an invitation arrived from the royal palace. "There's to be a ball," the stepmother read. "Every eligible maiden is to attend."

"Why, I can go, too!" Cinderella cried.

Her stepmother agreed, if Cinderella managed to finish her work. Gus and Jaq

and the other mice and birds decided to
surprise Cinderella. They sewed a lovely
gown while she worked at her chores.

3

Cinderella was overjoyed to find the
beautiful dress in her attic room. She put it
on and rushed to join her stepsisters.

"Look! That's my sash!" cried one in a
jealous rage.

"Those are my beads!" shrieked the
other. They tore at Cinderella's dress until it
was tattered and ruined. Poor Cinderella ran
to the garden in despair.

As she wept, Cinderella became aware of a gentle hand stroking her hair and a soft voice speaking to her.

"Who are you?" Cinderella asked the kindly woman.

"Why, I'm your fairy godmother, child," the woman said. "I've come to help you get to the ball." Then, with a wave of her wand, the mice changed into horses and a pumpkin became a glittering coach.

Cinderella was speechless. With another wave of her wand, the Fairy Godmother changed Cinderella's raggedy dress to a beautiful, shimmering gown. Cinderella looked down—she was even wearing sparkling glass slippers!

"You must leave the ball before midnight," the Fairy Godmother told her, "for then the spell will be broken."

As soon as Cinderella entered the ball, the Prince could not take his eyes off her. They danced under the light of the moon, and before long, they had fallen in love.

4

Suddenly, a chime sounded from high
above. The clock had begun to strike the
midnight hour. "I must go!" Cinderella
cried as she ran from the ballroom.

DISK 2
5

In her hurry, one glass shoe slipped
from her foot.

The Prince picked up the delicate
slipper. "I will marry the maiden whose
foot fits this slipper," he declared.

The Grand Duke and his footman set
out at dawn to find the owner of the glass

slipper. In time, they came to Cinderella's house and were both relieved to see that the glass slipper fit neither of the unpleasant stepsisters.

6

What the Grand Duke did not know was that Cinderella had been locked away in the attic by her evil stepmother. Gus and Jaq bravely stole the key and slid it under the door to free Cinderella just in time.

Just as the Grand Duke and his footman
were preparing to leave with the slipper,
Cinderella called to him. "Your Grace!
Please wait. May I try it on?"

The wicked stepmother sneered, but
there was nothing she could do. Or was

there? Just as the footman passed her, she tripped him with her cane. The glass slipper flew from his hands and shattered at Cinderella's feet.

The Grand Duke gasped in dismay. Just then, Cinderella spoke, "But you see, I have the other slipper." She held out the matching shoe to the delight of the Grand Duke and the horror of her stepmother. It fit her foot perfectly!

Cinderella's dreams had come true! The Prince and Cinderella were married right away, and they lived happily ever after.

7

8

The Little Mermaid

Under the sea, a royal concert was about to begin. King Triton had invited all the merpeople to hear his youngest daughter, Ariel, sing with her sisters. Sebastian the crab had great confidence in Ariel's debut, and his chest swelled with pride as a clamshell popped open to reveal . . . nothing. Ariel had forgotten about the concert!

Instead, she was busy exploring the wreck of a sunken ship with her fish friend Flounder. They suddenly got a big surprise.

DISK 1

"Shark!" Flounder shouted in a panic. Ariel and Flounder escaped just in time.

But they weren't entirely out of danger. The evil sea witch Ursula had been watching them from a magic bubble. Ursula hated King Triton and began to plot against him. "King Triton's daughter may be very useful to me," Ursula decided.

King Triton was furious about Ariel missing the concert. When he found out she had been up to the surface of the sea, he was angry. The king believed that the surface was a dangerous place. He put Sebastian in charge of keeping Ariel out of trouble.

Ariel swam to her hidden grotto. "I wish I could know what it would be like to live on land," she sighed. She had treasures that she had collected from sunken ships, but they only gave her a glimpse of what humans were really like.

Ariel looked up to see the shadow of a ship overhead. "Ariel, wait!" cried Sebastian,

but it was too late. Ariel swam to the ship.

Ariel watched as sailors sang and danced on the ship. She couldn't help noticing a handsome young man among them.

"Happy birthday, Prince Eric," said an older man, as he unveiled a statue of the dashing prince.

Suddenly, a storm blew in. Lightning flashed and the wind howled. Ariel watched as the ship tossed in the waves. Prince Eric was thrown overboard!

Ariel dove under the water and pulled the unconscious prince to shore. She had never been so close to a human before. She sang

to him softly until he began to wake up. Just then, a dog's barking startled her, and she quickly slipped back into the sea.

"There was a girl," the prince told his friend, Sir Grimsby. "She had the most beautiful voice. She saved me." He had fallen in love with the mysterious young woman.

Ariel had fallen in love, too. King Triton noticed how happy she was, but when he learned that she had disobeyed him and saved a human, he lost his temper. With one wave of his arm, King Triton destroyed all of Ariel's treasures in her grotto.

Ariel was quite upset with her father.

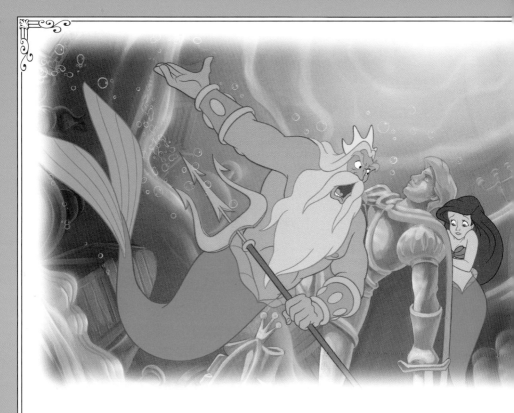

*He doesn't understand me or that I must follow my
own heart. And my heart leads me to Prince Eric.
I must see the prince again,* Ariel thought, *even if
I have to go to Ursula to do it!*

Ursula told Ariel that she could become
human for three days. By the end of that
time, the prince would have to give her a
kiss if she were to remain with him always,
or she would become a mermaid again.

"Oh, yes, we must talk about the
price. You must give me . . . your voice!"
Ursula cackled.

Ariel knew that Ursula could not be trusted, but she longed to be with Prince Eric once more. She signed the agreement. Immediately, her tail turned into legs, and she could no longer breathe underwater. She swam to the surface, gasping for air. When Ariel reached the shallow waters offshore, she gazed in wonder at her new legs.

Ariel discovered that life on land was even more exciting than she had ever dreamed.

Prince Eric was enchanted with Ariel. He invited her to stay at the palace and took her for a tour of the kingdom. Ariel wanted to let him know who she really was. Time was running out!

Flounder, Sebastian, and Scuttle the seagull tried to help the romance along. Sebastian sang a love song as Prince Eric leaned over to kiss Ariel. Suddenly, their boat tipped over! Flotsam and

Jetsam, Ursula's pet eels, had ruined the
lovely moment.

"That was too close," Ursula decided.
She came ashore disguised as a beautiful
woman to distract Eric. Using Ariel's voice,
she tricked the prince into thinking that she
was the one who had rescued him.

"We will be married today," Eric said,
taking the hand of his bride-to-be. Ariel
was heartbroken. She sat on the dock and
watched as the wedding ship sailed off into
the sunset.

Scuttle flew over the ship and recognized
Ursula on board. When Ariel learned the

true identity of the woman Eric planned to marry, she had to stop the wedding.

As the ceremony began, seagulls attacked the wedding party. The shell which held Ariel's voice was torn from Ursula's neck. Ariel's voice escaped and returned to Ariel.

"Eric!" Ariel cried. Ursula's spell was broken. The prince realized that Ariel was the woman who had saved him. He leaned forward to kiss her.

"You're too late!" shrieked Ursula. She grabbed Ariel, who had turned back into a mermaid, and pulled her under the water.

3

King Triton tried to stop Ursula from taking his daughter. "Take me instead," he said. Ursula agreed. With the king's trident in hand, she became huge.

Then suddenly Prince Eric steered the bow of the ship right into Ursula, putting an end to her forever.

When King Triton saw how deeply Ariel and Eric loved each other, he knew he had no choice but to grant them their wish to be married. He changed Ariel back into a human, and with humans and merpeople looking on, Ariel and Eric were married at sea. At last, Ariel's dreams had come true!